S0-ANO-786

RUBY CELEBRATES!
The Not-Quite-Perfect Passover

Laura Gehl

illustrated by
Olga and Aleksey Ivanov

Albert Whitman & Company
Chicago, Illinois

"There's good news and bad news," Dad tells Ruby. "Which do you want first?"

"The good news!" Ruby shouts.

"Bubbe can't host the first seder this year, since she broke her leg..." Dad begins. "So we are going to host."

"Yay!" Ruby cheers. "What's the bad news?"

"WE are going to host," Dad says again. He laughs at Ruby's expression. "It's going to be a lot of work."

"Let's start now!" Ruby says. "We need to plan the menu and clean the house and make invitations and..."

"One thing at a time," Dad says with a chuckle.

"Bubbe's been so sad since she broke her leg," Ruby says. "She can't ride her bike or go to dance class. And Passover is Bubbe's favorite holiday. We need to make Passover perfect to cheer her up!"

Ruby plans...

"No, Benny!" Ruby sighs.

Ruby cleans...

"No, Benny!" Ruby
stomps her feet.

Ruby cooks...

"NO, Benny!" Ruby yells as
she makes a diving catch.

Dad plops on the couch. Ruby draws invitations to send to her grandparents, aunts, uncles, cousins...and even cousin Ethan's dog, Boaz.

"Done!" she tells Dad. "I'll get the stamps and then do the envelopes."

But Ruby can't find stamps anywhere. And when she comes back...

"No, Benny!" Ruby screams.

"We'll never get everything perfect for Bubbe," she wails.
"And it's all Benny's fault!"

Ruby starts to cry.

Ruby curls up on the couch and pulls
a blanket over her head.

A small hand appears.

"Go away," Ruby says.

When Ruby hears Benny's footsteps walking out of the room, she rewrites the invitations. She addresses the envelopes. She puts on the stamps.

"Wait," Dad says, looking over Ruby's shoulder. "That's not the right date for the seder. And the stamps need to go on the *right-*hand corner."

Ruby dives back under the blanket. Passover will never be perfect for Bubbe. And it isn't just Benny's fault—it's her fault too.

"We can call everyone instead," Dad says.

"We can't call Boaz." Ruby sniffles.

"Ethan will tell him," Dad replies, chuckling.

Then the hand appears again.

Ruby throws off the blanket...and smiles.

"Thanks for bringing me BunBun, Benny. I know you've just been trying to help."

Pulling her brother into a hug, Ruby says, "I guess we won't have the most perfect Passover ever. But...maybe we can cheer up Bubbe anyway."

The next day, Ruby finishes cleaning...

during Benny's naptime.

When Benny wakes up, Ruby says he can chop apples for the charoset.

"How about a task for Benny that doesn't involve a knife?" Dad suggests.

So Ruby lets Benny add the spices.

Oops!

Ruby also finds the right job for Benny to do during the seder.

"You can throw these when we read about the plagues."

Everything is ready when the first guest arrives.

Almost.

Avital brings macaroons, and Uncle Jake hands Ruby a big box of chocolate-covered matzo.

Ethan comes in with Boaz on a leash.

Bubbe hobbles through the door on her crutches. "I love the decorations!"

During the seder, Benny does his job...

"Benny!" Ruby shrieks. "Where did you find a *real* frog?"

Everyone laughs.

Benny, Avital, Ruby, and Ethan search and search for the afikomen.

"We can't find it," Avital says. "It's nowhere!"

Then Ruby notices something.

"Boaz ate the afikomen!" Ruby yells.

Dad snorts. "Boaz is helping us have a not-quite-perfect Passover too."

"We've never laughed so much during Passover before," Bubbe says after she kisses Ruby good night. "Next year, do you think you can help *me* host a not-quite-perfect seder?"

Ruby grins. "Sure! But the helper you really need to make your seder not-quite-perfect is..."

"Benny."

A Note about Passover

Passover is a spring holiday that lasts for seven or eight days and commemorates the Exodus, how the Jewish people were freed from slavery in Egypt. On the first one or two nights of Passover, Jewish people celebrate with a festive ritual called a seder, which means "order" in Hebrew.

At the seder, Jews read, sing, eat, and pray. A special book called a Haggadah gives the order of the seder meal, which includes retelling the Exodus story. Foods eaten include matzo, haroseth (a mixture of fruit, nuts, and wine), maror (bitter herbs, such as horseradish), and parsley dipped in salt water. Each food is symbolic. Matzo, a thin unleavened bread, is eaten to remind us that the Jews had to leave Egypt so quickly that their bread did not have time to rise. The parsley symbolizes springtime, while salt water represents the tears shed by Hebrew slaves in Egypt.

During the part of the story in which God sends plagues to Egypt, some families involve young children by letting them throw small toys that represent each plague, just as Ruby suggests for Benny. While nobody wishes to make light of the suffering the plagues caused, this activity can be the starting point for age-appropriate discussions. At one point in the seder, a piece of matzo called the afikomen is hidden. Children search for the afikomen and often receive a prize for finding it.

Although seders are traditionally held on the first one or two nights of Passover, Jewish families commonly do not eat leavened foods, such as bread, for the full seven or eight days of the holiday.

Just as in this book Passover is Bubbe's favorite holiday, it is the favorite holiday for many Jews in real life. While seders are never perfect, they are usually bubbling with conversation, singing, laughter, and delicious matzo ball soup.

For Fred, Josh, and Debbie Edelman, and in memory of Ivy Edelman,
with much love—LG

To all children, who like to celebrate!—OI & AI

Library of Congress Cataloging-in-Publication data
is on file with the publisher.

Text copyright © 2023 by Laura Gehl
Illustrations copyright © 2023 by Albert Whitman & Company
Illustrations by Olga and Aleksey Ivanov
First published in the United States of America in 2023 by Albert Whitman & Company
ISBN 978-0-8075-7169-9 (hardcover)
ISBN 978-0-8075-7170-5 (ebook)
All rights reserved. No part of this book may be reproduced or transmitted
in any form or by any means, electronic or mechanical, including photocopying,
recording, or by any information storage and retrieval system,
without permission in writing from the publisher.

Printed in China
10 9 8 7 6 5 4 3 2 1 WKT 26 25 24 23 22

For more information about Albert Whitman & Company,
visit our website at www.albertwhitman.com.

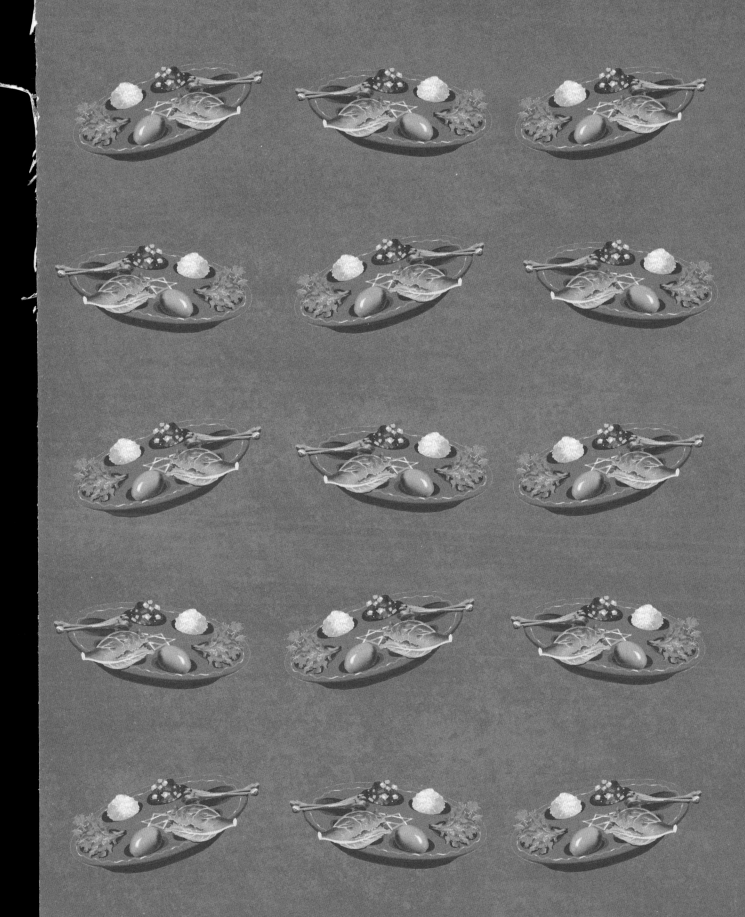